MW01100923

HAPPY BIRTHDAY TO ME

TO ME

Anne & Harlow Rockwell

MACMILLAN PUBLISHING COMPANY   NEW YORK

Macmillan Publishing Company
866 Third Avenue, New York, N.Y. 10022
Collier Macmillan Canada, Ltd.
Printed in Hong Kong

10 9 8 7 6 5 4 3

Library of Congress Cataloging in Publication Data

Rockwell, Anne F.   Happy birthday to me.
  Summary: A young child celebrates his birthday.
[1. Birthdays—Fiction] I. Rockwell, Harlow. II. Title.
PZ7.R5943Hap [E] 81-3738 ISBN 0-02-777680-8 AACR2

Look what a big boy I am!
Today is my birthday.
And I am having a party.

I help make my cake.
It is chocolate inside
and white frosting outside.

I blow up lots of red
and blue and yellow balloons.

I fill paper baskets
with nuts and gumdrops
and raisins.

My father writes the names
of my friends on the place cards.
He can write better than I can
because he is bigger.

I set the table
all by myself.
At every place I put
a little toy animal,

so my friends will have
a present on my birthday, too.
I get dressed in my best clothes.
Now I am all ready for my party.

Here come my friends.
They all have presents
for me.

We play
Pin the Tail on the Donkey.
Uh-oh!
Michael put the donkey's tail
on its nose.

We hunt for peanuts
in the living room.

Lizzy finds the most.

Then I open my presents.

Look at all the things I got!

My friends and I
sit down at the table.
We put on funny hats
and blow paper whistles
that make funny noises.

I take a big, deep breath.
I make a wish.
Then I blow out all the candles
with one big puff.
Now my wish will come true.
But I won't tell anyone
what I wished.
That is a secret.

The cake and ice cream are so good.
I had two helpings,
but Robert had three.

Then my friends take their
baskets of gumdrops, nuts
and raisins, their paper whistles,
their toy wild animals and
the peanuts they found.
They put them into bags.
They hold on to their
red, blue and yellow balloons,

and say good-by to me.
I say good-by and thank you, too.
This was the best birthday party
I ever had.